BEST HORSE
ON THE FORCE

BEST HORSE
ON THE FORCE

 Sherry Garland

PELICAN PUBLISHING COMPANY
GRETNA 2006

Names, characters, and events in this book are fictitious.
Any resemblance to actual events or persons, living or dead,
is purely coincidental.

First published by Henry Holt and Company, Inc., 1991
Published simultaneously in Canada by Fitzhenry and Whiteside Ltd., 1991
First Pelican edition, 2006

Library of Congress Cataloging-in-Publication Data

Garland, Sherry.
  Best horse on the force / Sherry Garland
  Summary: When Brandon and Wayne try to take revenge on a rookie
mounted policeman who has been teasing them, their practical joke backfires
and causes their favorite horse Skyjacker to be kicked off the force for cow-
ardice.
    ISBN-13: 978-1-58980-437-1 (pbk.)
    [1. Horses—Fiction. 2. Practical jokes—Fiction.] I. Title.
PZ7.G18415Be   1991
[Fic]—dc20   90-21048

Printed in the United States of America

Published by Pelican Publishing Company, Inc.
1000 Burmaster Street, Gretna, Louisiana 70053

Special thanks to the members of the Houston Police Mounted Patrol for their generous assistance

Contents

THE NEW HORSE

Why do people call those little tricks they play "practical jokes"? There's nothing practical about them. And sometimes they can end up causing a lot more trouble than they're worth. I learned that the hard way last summer. I still shiver when I think about the way things happened and how they turned out.

It was May the twenty-fifth, and everybody was already counting down the days until school would let out. When the final bell rang that afternoon, my best friend, Wayne, and I raced our bikes to the horse stables, ten blocks away. I pedaled as fast as I could, but Wayne beat me again.

Even though we were both twelve years old, and I was two inches taller and stronger than he was, Wayne was better at sports than me—and all the other boys in sixth grade. And I *was* ahead of Wayne for a while, until he took a shortcut through the bayou. He could have ruined his bike tires, and there was a big sign that said KEEP OUT! But that didn't stop Wayne. Nothing ever scared him.

We jumped off our bikes and leaned them against a white wooden arch that read HOUSTON POLICE MOUNTED PATROL. It was a hot spring day, so most of the horses that weren't out on patrol were in the paddocks soaking up the warm sunshine. A couple of them trotted up to the fence and whinnied when they saw us.

Helping out at the stables after school had been Wayne's idea when he found out my uncle was the trainer. Some of the work was disgusting, like shoveling manure out of the stalls. But grooming and feeding the horses was fun. Wayne had never even sat on a horse before, but now he rode like a pro.

We heard a noise and saw my uncle Roy over

in the round pen. He was riding a new horse, a shiny big chestnut with a light mane and tail. From the look of his long legs and powerful muscles, I figured he must have been a jumper. Uncle Roy was clicking his tongue and forcing the horse to make circle eights, then step sideways, then walk backward. Some horses don't like to back up, and resist it, but this big red horse was smart. He did everything my uncle commanded without any complaints.

"Hey, Uncle Roy." I waved and climbed up on the fence.

"Hello, Brandon. Howdy, Wayne. How do you like the new horse? He's a real dandy, isn't he?"

Uncle Roy pressed his knees against the horse's sides and steered him over to the fence.

"He sure is a dandy," Wayne said. "What's his name?"

"The man who donated him called him Skyjacker. Said he jumps so high, he looks like he's sailing through the air."

Skyjacker acted as if he knew we were talking about him. He cracked his mane like thunder and snorted. Then he stuck his nose right against my chest and shoved so hard, I almost fell off the fence.

Uncle Roy grinned and slapped the red neck with affection.

"I think he likes you, Brandon. Maybe you'd like to ride him."

I didn't know what to say. Uncle Roy knew I didn't ride horses. It wasn't that I was afraid of them. Not exactly. I liked to pet, groom, and feed them. I used to ride horses once, until I got hurt pretty bad when one ran away with me. I still got uneasy just thinking about it, and I wasn't in a hurry to try *that* again any time real soon.

"Which officer is going to get to ride Sky-jacker?" Wayne asked.

"I've been thinking I'll assign him to Chris Parker. His mount is going to retire soon. Chris has been pestering me for a horse with more pep."

Wayne rolled his eyes over toward me, and we both moaned. Chris Parker was the newest policeman on the mounted patrol. He had a baby face, curly hair, and freckles on his nose. The first time I met him, I thought he was still a teenager. He was really twenty-four years old, but he acted more like my sixteen-year-old cousin. It wasn't that Chris wasn't okay, exactly; he just had the weirdest sense of humor, which was mostly practical jokes. And Wayne and I were his favorite targets.

"Poor Skyjacker," Wayne mumbled under his breath. I agreed, and stroked the white blaze running down the horse's forehead. I wouldn't wish Chris on any horse, especially one as nice as this.

"When are you going to take Skyjacker through the first stress-training course?" I asked Uncle Roy.

"Tomorrow afternoon."

Wayne was straddling the fence, pulling green acorns off an oak tree and chunking them at a squirrel. Suddenly he sat up.

"Can we help out? Can I fire the gun?"

"We'll see, Wayne. Show up tomorrow right after school."

Wayne grinned and leaped down. We loved watching the crowd-control training course. That's when all the spare cops, and their friends, neighbors, and relatives, would get together to form a simulated crowd. We'd mill around the horse, shoving him, shouting, making loud noises, honking horns, and tossing Nerf balls at his face. A lot of the horses were just too nervous to go through all that, and would balk and shake and get all walleyed. Even the best of the horses got a little twitchy. But the real test, the one humdinger that all the horses had to pass, was the firecrackers and guns shooting out blank bullets. A horse that could stand that was a real champion police horse. I knew that Uncle Roy wouldn't let Wayne handle a real gun, even if all it had was blanks. But he might let us light a few of the firecrackers. As for me, I didn't want to go anywhere near a gun.

"Better get on inside and see what chores Smitty has for you boys today. I'll see you tomorrow." Uncle Roy tipped his hat and clicked to Skyjacker, making him back away from the fence to the middle of the corral.

"It's a shame that horse has to be wasted on Chris Parker," Wayne said. "I can tell he's going to be a super police horse."

I agreed, and looked at the beautiful horse over my shoulder as I climbed down the fence and walked toward the stables.

"He's going to be the best horse on the force. I betcha he passes the test tomorrow with flying colors."

2

IT AIN'T FUNNY

Smitty, the stable manager, was sitting in a cane-back chair leaning up against the wall. At his feet a banged-up portable radio was playing country-western music. Smitty was the only other civilian who worked at the mounted patrol besides me and Wayne.

A baseball cap was pulled down low over Smitty's gray hair, and his mouth was wide open, so we figured he was asleep. We walked down the rows of empty stalls to the tack room to get a currycomb and brush. The first thing we saw when we stepped inside the room was Chris Parker. He was still in his dark-blue riding breeches, a light-blue shirt, and knee-high black boots.

"Well, well, if it isn't the peewee policemen," he mocked. His grin always flashed from ear to ear, and I swear his teeth were as big as his horse's.

"Chris!" Wayne gasped. "What are you doing here so early? You're not supposed to come back until four thirty."

"Old Trooper turned up lame about an hour ago. I was checking out a call about that Ponytail Bandit. He hit another convenience store over on Westcott Street. I told Roy that old nag wasn't going to last much longer. Guess I'll be getting the new mount sooner than I thought."

Chris heaved his saddle up onto its rack, alongside the others. He was small for a policeman and grunted when he lifted the thirty-two pounds of gear.

"Say, boys, do me a favor and unbridle that poor old horse for me. I'm all pooped out from walking around so much."

Wayne looked at me and gave his secret hand signal—the same one Mr. Spock used on *Star Trek*. That always meant watch out. We had to be on our toes whenever Chris asked us to do anything. We never knew when it would turn into a joke, so we had developed a system of watching each other's back. While Wayne stepped out of the tack room, I walked out behind him backward, keeping my eyes on Chris.

Chris just shook his head and grinned again.

"You know, you two are paranoid. I think you ought to see a psychiatrist."

"We don't need a doctor," Wayne barked over his shoulder. "We know what's wrong . . . and we've got a cure. Get rid of you and all our problems would be solved." Wayne would say anything to anybody. He didn't care what people thought, but sometimes he just made things worse.

But Chris just laughed louder. He kind of rocked back on his boot heels, and his dark-brown eyes twinkled. That always meant trouble.

I watched Wayne's back while he unbridled the tired-looking older horse. When we came back into the tack room, Chris was sitting on a stool, wiping beads of sweat off his face with his handkerchief.

"Man, it's really starting to feel like summer

out there. Here, boys, help me get my boots off. I don't think I can stand to drive all the way home today with these tired dogs."

Wayne gave me the secret signal again as we knelt down and each grabbed a boot and tugged with all our might. Wayne's boot came off right away, but mine was stuck, so Wayne helped me pull it free.

"Man, I'm so dog-tired today. I sure dread driving all the way home in that old rattletrap pickup."

"Don't you have the air conditioner fixed yet, Chris?" I asked, remembering the last time I'd ridden in his truck, and nearly burned up.

"Nope. I'm waiting for the oil well in my backyard to start pumping. Should be any day now; then it's caviar and champagne for me. No more hot feet."

"*You* don't have an oil well in your backyard, Chris," Wayne said.

"Sure I do. Drilled it over the weekend." His face looked all serious for a minute, then he slapped his knee and smiled. "Ah, shoot, you're getting too smart for me, Wayne. Guess I can't fool you like I used to, huh?" He reached over to run his hand over Wayne's short hair, but Wayne ducked and stepped back.

"That's right, Chris. So why don't you give up trying?"

Chris just leaned back against the wall, then pointed toward a silver-colored cylinder standing next to the mini ice chest that held his lunch.

"Man, I dread that long hot drive. Do me a favor and fill my thermos bottle with water from the cooler."

I saw a light go off in Wayne's eyes as he picked up the thermos jug, and I could see he was biting his lip to keep from smiling. He grabbed my arm and pulled me out the door.

"Now's our chance to get even with Chris for that last joke he pulled on us," Wayne whispered.

"Whata ya mean? How?"

"You saw how hot Chris is. He's craving a cool drink. So instead of filling the thermos with water from the cooler, all we have to do is fill it with water from the hot-water faucet."

I started to laugh, but Wayne shushed me.

"You go to the cooler and make some noise,

and make sure he hears the gurgle. I'll sneak out to the wash area and get some hot water."

I strolled to the water cooler. It was one of those big clear-plastic bottles turned upside down and attached to an electric cooling device. I whistled and pretended to be talking to Wayne, and ran enough water so that big bubbles gurgled up.

The thought of finally getting revenge on Chris was filling up my brain. I imagined him on the highway, stuck in the rush-hour traffic in his un-air-conditioned pickup, sweat streaming down his face and all over his curly hair. He reaches over for the thermos jug, his mouth dry as cotton and aching for a cool drink of water. His eyes stare ahead at the traffic as he fishes for the bottle on the seat. His heart is thankful for those two wonderful boys who filled it up. He unscrews the lid, lifts the silver flask to his parched lips, takes a deep swig, then . . .

"Aaaaaugh!"

A shout like bloody murder hit the roof and echoed through the stables. I dropped the paper cup in my hand and ran down the breezeway. At first I couldn't see because the light was so bright.

Then I heard the familiar high-pitched laughter of Chris Parker and saw him coming out of the tack room.

Then I heard Wayne scream again; only this time he was yelling out every cussword he knew. I followed the sound toward the outside wash area where we scrub down the horses. Wayne was on the ground, sitting in a puddle of muddy water and a big pile of horse manure. All around him were those big weird-looking red-and-green-and-yellow artificial snakes—the kind people stuff down inside a can. The silver thermos was lying over beside the water faucet.

"He did it again," I sighed with disgust, and walked over to give Wayne a hand up. Chris's laughter grew louder, until he was standing only a few feet away.

"You were supposed to get the water from the cooler. But this . . . this is even better. Look at your pants." Chris pointed, then doubled over and broke into another fit of laughter.

Wayne would never tell Chris in a million years why he was at the hot-water faucet. His face turned beet red, and he slipped a couple of times in the mud before he could get up. I knew better than to say a word, but just looked up at Chris and shook my head in disgust. Then I took out after Wayne, who had already run out the other end of the stables, dodging past Smitty, who was on his way to see what the commotion was about.

AFTERSHOCKS

"What in tarnation's going on around here!" Smitty yelled.

"Oh, just the usual. Chris played another trick on Wayne."

"Dad blast it! When's that young pup going to grow up and start acting like a man?"

Even in his cowboy boots, Smitty wasn't much taller than me. And he was almost as skinny, too. But he was one of the strongest men I knew. He could lift a thirty-two-pound saddle without flinching and heave a bale of hay like it was nothing.

"Go get Wayne and I'll wash him off. He

smelled worse than a scared skunk when he ran by here."

I trotted out of the stables to the place where we had left the bikes. Wayne's bicycle wasn't there, but his blue jeans were—all covered with mud and horse manure and tossed aside into the bushes. I cringed just thinking about poor Wayne riding down the street in his underwear. Even though he was wearing one of those shirts with extra-long tails, I could just imagine what he was mumbling under his breath.

I found an old piece of broken tree limb and used it to pick up the jeans, holding my nose while I carried them over to Smitty. I helped him rinse the pants off thoroughly at the washdown area.

In a few minutes Chris Parker came out of the tack room, dressed in his civilian clothes, rolling up his shirt sleeves.

"Where's Wayne?" he asked.

"Don't know," Smitty snapped. "Reckon the boy ran away. Can't say I blame him. That was a mean trick you played on him. Just about ruined his good breeches."

Smitty pointed the hose nozzle at a spot of mud on the concrete slab and swished it down the drainage grate.

Chris ran his fingers through his curly hair, then hissed air through his teeth.

"Okay, okay. You're right, Smitty. But I didn't know he was going to go out to the wash area to get the water. I told him to go to the water cooler. It's nice and clean in there. Shoot, it was just a few plastic snakes. I didn't expect to cause so much trouble."

"Well, that's your problem," Smitty grumbled as he tossed the hose aside and turned off the faucet. "You don't ever think 'bout what might happen when you play one of your little jokes."

"Okay, okay, man." Chris held up both hands and stepped back a foot. "I'll apologize to the little stinker the next time I see him. Will that make you happy?" Chris slapped Smitty on the shoulder, but the old man just glared at the hand until Chris took it off.

"By the looks of Wayne's reaction, I'd say the boy may not be coming back here again," Smitty said.

Both of the men looked at me, and I didn't know what to say. I hoped it wasn't true. I couldn't imagine coming to the stables without my best friend. I loved to take care of the horses, but I would feel like some kind of traitor if I came alone.

Why couldn't Chris just be a normal person? I wondered. And why couldn't Wayne have just left things alone? If he hadn't been trying to play a trick on Chris in the first place he wouldn't have ended up in the mud and manure.

After Chris left, I helped Smitty bring in the horses from the paddocks and pour feed into their stall buckets. In a few minutes Uncle Roy brought in the new horse, Skyjacker, and asked me to cool him down, then give him a good brushing.

Skyjacker was something else. He did everything I asked him to do as I led him around the paddock in his blanket. Now and then he would shove me with his nose, or act like he was trying to pick something out of my pocket. By the time I'd put him in his stall, poured him a bucket of feed, and brushed him down, I was convinced he was the smartest horse the police mounted patrol ever had.

I wanted to stay longer, but the officers were starting to bring in their mounts for the day, and it was time for me to get home. I wasn't sure if I should take Wayne's jeans to his house. By the time I could pedal there and then over to my apartment, it would be really late, and I would have to explain everything to my mom. Then she'd probably tell Wayne's mother, who would probably tell Uncle Roy, who would probably say something to Chris. . . . Who knew where it would all end?

If I knew Wayne, he didn't want anybody to find out what had happened—especially his mom and dad, who had never liked the idea of us working at the stables after school anyway. Wayne's grades weren't so hot, and his mom was sure that if he'd spend more time studying instead of working around the police horses, his grades would be better. She agreed to let him do it only because I was tutoring him in math.

I rolled Wayne's wet jeans up into a tight little bundle and tied them with my belt, hoping nobody would notice them. I got real lucky, because Uncle Roy was pulling out of the drive in his pickup just at the time I was getting ready to leave. He offered to put my bike in the back and drop me off at Wayne's house.

"What happened to Wayne?" he asked as he shifted gears.

"Uh, he had to get home early to take care of something."

Uncle Roy looked at me kinda funny with his squinted eyes and leathery, tanned face, but didn't press me. He was that kind of man. Didn't talk much, and I never saw him lose his temper even once, with man or horse. But that didn't mean he was easy. I saw him fire more than one stable hand for doing a poor job.

He didn't say another word, but that was okay with me, because I was thinking about Wayne. As the truck rumbled down the street, I could almost see Wayne riding along the bike trail, zooming past the intersection with his shirttails flying, his bare legs looking all pale because we hadn't been swimming yet this year.

After Uncle Roy dropped me off, I went inside

Wayne's house. His mother wasn't home from work yet, but Wayne's little sister, Sandy, and one of her ugly girlfriends were watching TV. As soon as I walked through the door, Sandy started firing questions at me.

"What happened to Wayne's pants? Why's he locked in his room? Why'd he yell at me and Cindy?"

Sandy kept on blabbering, and I wanted to put tape over her big mouth, but I just pushed her aside and climbed up the stairs to Wayne's room. The door was locked and he didn't answer when I called out, so I just unrolled his jeans and slung them over the curtain rod in the bathroom. I called later that night, but his dad said he was asleep.

I didn't see Wayne until the next morning. The first thing he said when he came out the door, holding his math book in one hand and a Pop-tart in the other, was: "I know how to get even with Chris Parker once and for all. This time I *know* it's going to work."

REVENGE

I prodded Wayne all day long to tell me what he had in mind, but he kept his trap shut for once in his life. He just kept on saying, "Revenge is sweet." Then he'd grin and get a terrible glint in his eyes that gave me chill bumps.

We got out of school early because of a teacher's meeting and pedaled like crazy to the police-horse stables. When we got there, Wayne reached into his shirt pocket and pulled out a wad of blue toilet tissue.

"What's that for?" I asked.

"This is the answer to all our problems," he

said as he carefully unwrapped the tissue. "I found this on the way home yesterday."

There, lying on the palm of his hand, was *the* biggest, *the* ugliest, *the* sharpest cocklebur I'd ever laid eyes on. I couldn't help but whistle.

"Wow! That's wicked looking." I reached over and touched one of the barbs, and it stuck like a needle. A little speck of blood popped up on my fingertip.

"Yeah. It's perfect for Chris Parker."

I chuckled. I could just see Wayne dropping it down one of Chris's boots. The young cop would probably scream like a stuck pig half the afternoon.

"That'll sure make Chris holler," I said. "But how are you going to slip it in his boot? It won't be any fun unless we can be there to see him."

"Boot? Who's talking about putting it in his boot? Nope, I've got better plans for this baby." He wrapped up the granddaddy cocklebur and carefully put it back in his shirt pocket.

"But—"

"Shhh! There goes Chris. Looks like they're

getting ready to start the stress-training course. We gotta hurry."

By the time we reached the big arena with the bleachers on two sides, Uncle Roy, Chris Parker, and several other policemen and civilians had formed a crowd. Each person had something in his hand—a Nerf ball, a horn, a balloon, or some kind of noisemaker. Uncle Roy had a pistol filled with blank bullets, one cop had a squirt gun, and another guy had driven two pickups into the arena and left the motors running.

We saw Smitty leading Skyjacker from the stables, already saddled up. Wayne ran over to him.

"Smitty, can we lead Skyjacker to the arena? Please?"

Smitty shifted a big wad of chewing tobacco from one cheek to the other, then nodded.

"Glad to see that little incident yesterday didn't do you any harm, Wayne," he said.

"Ah, forget it," Wayne said, and handed the reins to me. I stroked Skyjacker's face as we watched Smitty walk over to the arena. Wayne suddenly turned and whispered, "Now's our chance."

"What—"

My words sorta stuck in my throat when I saw Wayne work the cocklebur from his pocket, unwrap it, and slip it under the left side of the saddle blanket, just where the stirrup strap hung down. Skyjacker shivered his skin as if he'd been bitten by a horsefly, and sidestepped a little. But he didn't squeal, so I knew none of the barbs had really stuck him.

"Wayne, you're crazy! Chris will kill us if he catches us!"

"Don't worry." Wayne winked as he patted Skyjacker and took the reins from me. "I stayed up all night planning this. I know it's gonna work."

We joined the rest of the men in the arena. They were making an awful racket, shouting, whistling, honking, and milling about. Wayne handed the reins to Chris and grinned.

"Good luck, Chris."

"Say, Wayne-the-Pain, you're not still mad, are you?"

"Ah, forget it, Chris. I'm not sore at you."

"You're a good sport," Chris said, and rubbed

Wayne's hair. I felt a big rush of guilt when I thought about what was going to happen. But Wayne must have sensed my doubt, because he grabbed my arm and pulled me back before I could speak up.

Skyjacker didn't particularly like all the noise, but he was being real cool about it. Even when Chris climbed into the saddle, he didn't balk.

"Okay, Chris, bring him over this way!" Uncle Roy shouted. "I'm fixing to fire the blanks and light the firecrackers."

I felt Wayne's fingers digging into my arm, and I heard him suck in his breath. "This is it," he whispered. I just stuck my fingers in my ears and gritted my teeth.

Uncle Roy fired the gun into the air, and at the same time Chris pressed his legs against Skyjacker's sides.

Zoom! Skyjacker shot into the air like a rocket, then gave one big, twisting buck.

Sling! Chris Parker sailed through the air, his open mouth screaming and his arms and legs kicking.

Wham! Chris landed in the dirt, right on his face.

Wayne and I laughed so hard, big tears were rolling down our cheeks, and my side started to ache.

"Dad gummit!" Chris said as he climbed to his feet, spitting dirt and cussing. He grabbed his hat and jammed it down over his curly hair.

"Too much horse for you, Chris?" Smitty teased, then shot a stream of tobacco juice to the sand.

"Shoot! That dern horse acts like he's crazy. Bring that animal over here," Chris said as he limped toward Skyjacker, who had run to the far side of the arena.

"We'll go get him for you!" Wayne shouted, and bolted toward the horse before anybody could stop him. I ran after him and caught up just as Wayne was lifting the blanket.

"Quick, give me a leg up," Wayne said, and wiggled his foot into the stirrup.

"Don't get up there! You'll get tossed like a salad."

"I took the burr out; it's safe now." He opened

his hand and showed me the sticky weapon, which had already punctured little holes in his hand.

I shook my head, but did what he said. Chris and Uncle Roy scratched their heads when they saw Wayne riding up.

"There's nothing wrong with this horse," said Wayne. "Just needs the right kind of touch."

"Turn him to the right," Chris ordered. "Press your leg real hard."

Wayne squeezed his legs as hard as he could and made Skyjacker do all kinds of things. Chris took his hat off, scratched his head, then shrugged.

"Okay. Let's try again. Must have been a fluke."

Uncle Roy looked at Skyjacker's eyes, then pressed the saddle blanket all over. He didn't look very happy.

"Hmmm. I don't see anything wrong. I sure hope he's not gun shy. Get back up, Chris."

Wayne made Skyjacker walk a few feet away.

"Brandon, give me a hand down!" he shouted. I knew he didn't really need help, but I ran over anyway. He slipped the cocklebur into my hand while he pretended to get untangled from the stirrups. "Stick this under the blanket quick," he whispered.

"But, Wayne, they almost caught us."

"They checked and didn't find nothing. It's okay now. Hurry."

My fingers shook like a leaf as I put the cocklebur under the blanket, this time on the right side because that was where I was standing. Skyjacker's body was between me and the crowd. Wayne got off, making a big grunt and commotion so that everybody would be sure to watch him and not me. Then we led Skyjacker back.

"Wayne, I don't know. . . ." I started to whisper, but he twisted my arm and mumbled at me between clenched teeth.

It was worse than I thought. This time when Uncle Roy fired the blanks, Skyjacker bucked like a wild bronco, then took a big running leap right over the fence and the water trough.

Well, that was just perfect. Chris Parker lost his grip, screamed, and plopped straight into the water. He looked like a turtle on its back, with his legs and arms kicking. I know it's awful, but I couldn't help but laugh. Neither could Wayne, or Smitty. Even Uncle Roy's stone face cracked a smile.

Chris came up out of the trough spewing water, slipping and sliding as he tried to get his behind unstuck. It was better than a movie.

"I'm gonna kill that stupid horse!" He spat the words out right along with the dirty water.

"Go get Skyjacker before he gets into the street," Uncle Roy told me and Wayne. He had a funny look on his face, so I was glad to get out of the arena.

Wayne and I ran to where Skyjacker had stopped, over by the hay barn. Wayne took the cocklebur out, and Skyjacker seemed relieved, because he heaved a big sigh and pushed his muzzle against my chest. Wayne rewrapped the burr in the blue tissue paper.

"Wow. That was close," I said in a shaky voice.

"Yeah, but it was worth it to see Chris flying through the air."

We walked Skyjacker back to the arena, where Chris pretended to punch him in the face. Uncle Roy glanced at his watch.

"It's getting late. I think we'd better stop for now. Let's do it again tomorrow at two o'clock, if you don't mind coming over on Saturday, Chris. Boys, go put Skyjacker up and cool him down."

Wayne took the saddle off, then walked Skyjacker until he was cooled off. We ran a washrag over the spot where the burr had pricked his skin, so there was no evidence.

After we'd done a few more chores and climbed on our bikes, I said to Wayne, "We really were lucky we didn't get caught. You'd better throw that cocklebur in the bayou. You know, like they say—destroy the evidence."

But Wayne just grinned and shook his head.

"Nope. I don't think so yet. I like the way Chris looks sitting in the water trough."

"Wayne! We'd better not try it again. Our luck is gonna run out sometime."

"Are you turning chicken on me, Brandon?"

"Well, no. But haven't we gotten even with Chris?"

"Look—you didn't have to ride through the middle of rush-hour traffic in your underwear, like I did. You can't get much more humiliating than that, can you?"

I shrugged.

"Besides," Wayne continued, "I told you I've already planned this all out. We got away with it today, and tomorrow won't be any different. You are coming tomorrow, aren't you?"

"Ah, I can't. We're going to my grandparents' farm. We probably won't get back until after dark."

"Too bad," Wayne said as we started pedaling off. "I have a feeling this next time will cure Chris Parker of playing jokes on us once and for all."

"Are you gonna tell him you did it?"

"Sure. After just one more trick. This will be my last one. I promise."

As we came to the split in the road where Wayne turned left and I turned right, I waved good-bye. I had a funny feeling that his words were going to be more true than he suspected.

THE OTHER HORSE

The next morning, while it was still dark, my family piled into the car and drove to my grandparents' farm. My sister fell asleep, but I watched the scenery change from flatlands to rolling hills speckled with white-faced cattle and quarter horses. This time of the morning the horses were frisky, and ran about kicking up their heels. Some of the pastures had huge live-oak trees so big that a small herd of cattle could gather under one during the hottest part of the day.

We turned off the interstate and drove thirty more minutes down a narrow farm-to-market road before we saw my grandfather's homemade mailbox, shaped like a covered wagon. The car tires rattled as we drove over the cattle grate onto the private gravel road that led to the farmhouse, another mile away.

On both sides of the bumpy road, rows and rows of young green cotton plants stretched out as straight as arrows. Grandpa waved from the top of his tractor, and Mom honked the horn. In a pasture up ahead I saw dozens of cattle grazing. I looked around to see if I could find my grandfather's horse, Snipper. I wanted to make sure I didn't get too close to him. After what had happened the last time I tried to ride him, old Snipper and I weren't exactly on friendly terms.

"Get out!" Grandma shouted from the long, covered front porch where she was rocking and peeling potatoes. As usual, she squeezed the living daylights out of me, and then she turned my head sideways to examine the little scar on my left temple.

"Well, now, that scar healed up real nice, Brandon. If I didn't know where to look for it, I wouldn't even have noticed."

"Next thing you know, you'll want to get back

up on old Snipper and try again. Ain't that right?" Grandpa said as he climbed up the porch steps. He was wearing the same thing he always wore, a pair of gray-and-white-striped bib overalls and a worn-looking gray hat with a sweat stain all the way around the band. His hands smelled like chewing tobacco, and his walrus mustache scratched my cheeks when he hugged me.

"I'm not sure I want Brandon to ride that old horse again, Daddy," my mom said. I sighed with relief. Those motherly instincts could really come in handy sometimes.

"You know you gotta get back up on a horse when you fall off, or you'll never like to ride," Grandpa said.

I began to feel twitchy. All of a sudden this pleasant little Saturday visit was turning into more trouble. I almost wished I'd stayed home and gone to the police stables with Wayne. I sure hoped Wayne wasn't going to do anything crazy.

But I didn't get much of a chance to think about Wayne and Skyjacker, because as soon as we'd eaten lunch, Grandma gave metal buckets to me and my sister and sent us to the blackberry patch. She wanted us to fill the pails with berries so she could cook two cobbler pies—one to eat and one for us to take home.

"Y'all be sure to watch out for copperheads!" Grandma yelled out as we left.

The berry vines rambled all along the sides of a dried-up creek bed and around an old abandoned well. Big, juicy blackberries covered the vines, but so did tiny, sharp thorns.

"I betcha I can fill my bucket first," I said to my sister.

"Okay. How much?" she said as she popped a berry into her mouth.

"How about a dollar?"

"It's a deal." We shook on it, then scrambled to opposite sides of the berry vines. I knew I could beat her, until I saw her pull out an old pair of cloth garden gloves. Her fingers flew over the sticky, prickly vines. After a few minutes my hands looked like woodpecker bait. I glanced over and saw that she was getting ahead of me, so I asked myself: What would Wayne do in a situation like this?

The answer was easy. I picked up a stick, tossed it over into the vines not too far from my sister, and shouted: "Copperhead!"

She dropped that bucket and ran so fast she didn't even hear me laughing. In no time I filled my pail and hers. Then I shouted down the old well and listened to the echo, and dropped rocks down it to see how deep it was. I wished Wayne was here. I was sure he'd think of something fun to do with the well.

When I got back to the farmhouse, my sister wasn't speaking to me. She grabbed the buckets from my hands and refused to pay me the dollar she'd lost in the bet. I tried to watch TV, but the reception was so bad, it was like watching geese in a snowstorm. And the nearest town was so small, you could spit from one end to the other. No movie house, no video games, not even a Dairy Queen.

I decided to walk over to the pasture where Snipper was grazing. Snipper was a big gray horse that a neighbor had given to my grandpa two years ago when he'd had to sell his farm. Snipper

THE OTHER HORSE | 39

had black eyes and laid-back ears, and wasn't named Snipper for nothing.

Snipper saw me, threw his head up, and came galloping. My heart thumped as he charged at the fence, then churned to a halt in a cloud of dust. As soon as I tried to pet his gray nose, he lifted his lip and chomped at my fingers. I pulled up a handful of grass and held it out, but even that made me uneasy. He jerked the grass out of my hand and began chewing while his eyes rolled and glared at me.

"Wanna ride him?" Grandpa called from the barn door. "Got a saddle right here all ready." He walked toward us, saddle and bridle slung over his shoulder.

"No thanks, Grandpa. I've got some chores to do."

"Ah, don't worry about chores. We can do them later. Why don't we saddle old Snipper up and ride to the mailbox to see if there's any mail?"

"Uh, no thanks," I said.

Grandpa smiled, then put his hand on my shoulder.

"You know, everybody gets tossed now and then when they're learning to ride. It's nothing to be ashamed of. Happened to me lots of times. And your uncle Roy's bottom was nicely acquainted with the dirt."

I looked at Snipper's black eyes, then shrugged.

"Uh, maybe next time, Grandpa. I'm kinda tired right now."

Grandpa patted my shoulder.

"All right. Guess you need a little more time. But remember, not all horses are as mean as Snipper. He just doesn't like boys."

As Grandpa saddled and bridled the horse, Snipper shook his head, then pawed a trench in the ground. Then he glared at me.

No way! I hated to disappoint my grandfather, but me and that horse had nothing to say to each other.

Grandpa rode off down the dirt road toward the mailbox, and I went back inside and stared at the snowy TV until we got ready to leave. All the way home, I thought about what Grandpa had said, and wished I had at least tried to ride

Snipper one time. With Grandpa in the saddle too, probably nothing would have happened. I wished I could be more like Wayne. He wasn't afraid of anything.

I was in an awfully bad mood when we got home after dark, and all I wanted to do was make a beeline for my bedroom. But the phone was ringing when I came through the front door.

"Hello," I said.

"Brandon! Boy, am I glad you're finally home. I've been calling you all afternoon." Wayne's voice sounded funny.

"I told you we were going to the farm. What's up?"

"Man, are we in trouble," he said in a breathless voice, and I knew he had his hand cupped around the phone to keep somebody from hearing him, because suddenly his words got all jumbly.

"Wayne, I can hardly hear you," I complained. "What'd you say?"

"I put the cocklebur under the saddle again.

Skyjacker threw Chris Parker real bad this time. Chris was rushed to the hospital emergency room. I think he's—" Suddenly he stopped.

"Wayne!" I stammered, but I heard someone yelling at him, and he hung up.

DISGRACED

I called Wayne right back, but his dad answered and said he couldn't talk anymore. I got ready for bed, but I couldn't sleep. First I jerked the covers off; then I pulled them back on. I tossed to my right, then to my left, then on my back, then on my stomach. I stared at the ceiling; I stared out the window. But nothing would stop my brain from spinning.

I kept imagining Chris Parker tumbling through the air, landing on his head. I could see blood spurting all over him, then the ambulance screaming through the traffic to the hospital. Then I saw the doctor standing over Chris, shak-

43

ing his head, and pulling the sheet over Chris's face.

By six in the morning I'd hardly slept two hours and was standing in the hall, staring at the telephone. My fingers shook while I dialed Uncle Roy's home number.

"Yep," he said in a gravelly voice that hadn't cleared with a cup of coffee yet.

"Uncle Roy, this is Brandon."

"Brandon? You're up mighty early for a Sunday morning. Is something wrong?"

"Uh, nothing's wrong here. But Wayne told me that Chris Parker had an accident. Is he . . . ?" I swallowed real hard. "Is he all right?"

"Chris Parker? Oh, sure. Lucky thing for him he landed on his arm and not his head. Had a fracture, but nothing serious. He'll just pull office duty for a few weeks."

My sigh was so loud, I think the neighbors could have heard it.

"I'm sorry about Chris, Uncle Roy," I said.

"Well, these things happen. But I really misjudged that horse Skyjacker. I could have sworn he was perfect police-horse material. Just goes to show you."

It was then that I realized that Wayne must not have told anybody about the cocklebur prank. I said good-bye to Uncle Roy, got dressed, and rode my bike all the way to Wayne's house without even eating breakfast first.

"You didn't tell Uncle Roy about the cocklebur, did you?" I demanded as I stared down at Wayne, still curled up in his bedcovers, all droggy-eyed.

"What happened to you?" he asked, sitting up and rubbing his eyes. "Your eyes are all red and your hair's going every whichway."

"Did you or did you not tell anybody about the cocklebur?" I repeated.

Wayne shrugged, then flipped on his TV set with the remote control. "Not yet."

"You *have* to tell Uncle Roy. He thinks Skyjacker is uncontrollable. How can you just stand by and let that innocent horse take the blame for what happened?"

"I'll tell him. Later. After things have cooled down a little bit. You should have seen how mad

Uncle Roy was, and Chris was hollering that he was going to shoot Skyjacker. I think we'd better wait till Monday after school to tell them." Wayne flipped the channels so fast, they flew by in a blurr of color. Then he looked up at me and smiled. "Trust me, Brandon. It's best to stay away when folks are mad. I know all about it."

Well, that was probably true. Wayne did have a knack for getting in and out of trouble. I guess that made him an expert.

"Oh, all right. I guess it won't hurt to wait until Monday to tell."

Wayne wanted me to stay and play video games, but I went back home and piled into bed. I didn't even get my shoes off before I was in dreamland.

That Monday at school was a riot. It was the last week of school, and everyone was so-o-o-o impatient. I almost forgot about Skyjacker and our confession, but around two o'clock I began to worry again.

I pulled out a sheet of notebook paper and wrote up the best confession I could think of. In case Uncle Roy wasn't there, I'd just leave it on his desk. It said:

> TO WHOM IT MAY CONCERN,
> WE PUT A BURR UNDER SKYJACKER'S
> SADDLE. HE'S A GOOD HORSE AND
> DIDN'T MEAN TO ACT SO CRAZY.

I signed the note and passed it over to Wayne to sign. But then Mrs. Rainbolt, our teacher, grabbed it, read it, and made me and Wayne stand up and recite a dorky poem in front of the whole class. Afterward Wayne ignored me. When he did look my way, he shot out knives with his eyes.

"That was dumb," he finally said as we unchained our bikes after school. "You're lucky Mrs. Rainbolt didn't make you read the note out loud. Then the whole school would have known what happened."

"They're going to find out anyway when we confess," I said.

"Let's get it over with then. I expect that Uncle Roy will be so mad he won't ever let us work at the stables anymore. But if you're so hot for a confession, guess you won't mind."

"Not work at the stables? Gee, I never thought about that. You think he was *that* mad?"

"You didn't see his face. I never saw Uncle Roy swear or get mad before. But he did Saturday."

I felt uneasy. If Uncle Roy had lost his temper, it would have been the first time in my life. That wasn't a good sign.

Wayne glanced over at me. "Are you still sure you want to confess? Nothing will be gained by it anyhow."

"Just Skyjacker's reputation."

"Oh, they'll get over it. Next time they take Skyjacker through the test course, he'll pass with flying colors, and everybody will forget what happened."

When we rode under the white arch and propped up our bikes, I didn't see Uncle Roy in any of the paddocks or in the arena. His pickup wasn't in sight either.

We went inside the stable to look for Smitty and Skyjacker. All the horses were inside, because it was starting to sprinkle and the weatherman had predicted thunderstorms.

"Howdy, boys," Smitty said. "Just in time for your favorite sport—shoveling manure." He held out a big scooped shovel.

"Ugh," we both moaned.

"Guaranteed to build up great muscles. Just like mine." He flexed one of his skinny arms, then grinned.

While Smitty was talking, I was looking up and down the stables for Skyjacker. All the regular horses had brass nametags on their stall doors. Skyjacker, since he was new and not a certified police horse yet, usually stayed in a spare stall down at the end. But it was empty now.

I pretended to get a drink and walked up and down the breezeway, checking each stall. No Skyjacker.

"Looking for something, Brandon?" Smitty asked.

I whirled around.

"Uh . . . well . . . I just thought I'd say hello to Skyjacker. Don't tell me he's already out on the job?"

"Nope."

Wayne stepped up, a curious look on his face. "He's not out in the paddocks, is he?"

"Nope."

Wayne and I looked at each other. I had a creepy feeling all over.

"Smitty, just where is Skyjacker?"

"He's not here anymore."

"What! Where is he?"

"Your uncle Roy loaded him up in the horse trailer and hauled him back to the man who donated him. Skyjacker's been fired, dismissed, discharged. That horse is history now."

WHERE IS SKYJACKER?

"Why?" I yelped.

Smitty spat out his tobacco, then leaned on the shovel handle.

"That fool horse can't be trusted. He's gun shy. Scared senseless of loud noises. Every time he hears one, he goes berserk. He coulda killed Chris Parker Saturday, you know."

"But that's not true!" I shrieked. "It wasn't Skyjacker's fault. It was—"

Wayne grabbed my arm and twisted it.

"What Brandon means is that Skyjacker seemed like such a good horse. He just needs one more chance. We *know* he'll act right the next time."

"Roy already gave him three chances. Like they say—three strikes and you're out."

I was so mad at Wayne and his stupid cocklebur trick I could almost have cried. And I was mad at myself for not stopping him.

"When's Uncle Roy coming back?" I asked.

"He said he'd be out the rest of the day."

I stomped out of the stables, across the gravel parking lot, and toward the prefab building that served as the offices. Wayne came running after me.

"Hey, where're you going?" he called out.

"I'm going to leave Uncle Roy that confession. Then I'll call him tonight. I can't let Skyjacker take the blame for that accident. It's not right. He's a good horse—the best I've ever seen. He's smart, and gentle . . ."

"Okay, okay. But hold on a minute. Let me write it. After all, you weren't the one who put the cocklebur under the saddle. It was *me*. And it'll be *me* who gets in all the trouble."

I stopped in my tracks and thought a minute. I guessed he was right, mostly. The whole thing had been his idea, and I guessed he should be the one to confess. But I had just stood by and let him do it, so I didn't feel any less guilty.

"Okay," I said. "You can write the note the way you want. But I'll sign it too."

"Good. Let's go inside Uncle Roy's office and get some paper and a pen."

We stepped into the trailer, expecting to see Ginny, the policewoman who was on office duty this month. But instead of her usual pretty, smiling face, we saw the sour puss of Chris Parker. He was barking into the telephone, arguing like a baseball umpire.

"I'm gonna sue!" he snapped into the mouthpiece. "I'm gonna sue the fool who gave that horse to us. He said the horse was gentle, well trained, never got nervous about anything. I could have been killed." He glanced over at us and wiggled the fingers of the arm that was in a cast and a sling.

"Oh, brother," Wayne moaned as he pushed me into Uncle Roy's empty office. "This is getting hairier every minute. I didn't think Chris would be so mad."

"Can he really sue somebody for what happened?"

"Shoot, yeah. My dad says in America anybody can sue anybody else for anything. Don't you ever watch Judge Wapner on TV?"

Wayne's dad was a lawyer, so I guessed he knew what he was talking about. Suddenly I felt like there was a whole flock of butterflies flapping around inside my stomach.

"What's the matter, Brandon? Having second thoughts about confessing?" Wayne whispered as he rummaged around Uncle Roy's desk for a blank sheet of paper.

I nodded, and plopped down in Uncle Roy's big swivel chair, sinking into the padded leather.

"What are we going to do now, Wayne?"

"Let me think." He bit his lip and began pacing the floor, like he always did when he was figuring something out. Suddenly he jerked to a halt and held up one finger.

"I've got it! We'll find the man who donated Skyjacker, get him to fire off some blank bullets, and prove that Skyjacker is calm. We could say that Skyjacker must have been sick Friday and Saturday, or that we found a little sticker in his blanket. Maybe we won't have to confess."

"After Uncle Roy learns that Skyjacker isn't afraid of guns, he'll take him back. Great idea, Wayne."

We walked back out, where Chris was still arguing on the phone. When another line buzzed and lit up, he pushed the wrong buttons and lost both calls.

"Doggone it!" he snapped. "I hate this office work. Nothing makes sense. Can't find anything. I was just filling out a report on the Ponytail Bandit's latest holdup, and now it's gone." He began shuffling through a stack of papers.

"Ginny never has any trouble with phone calls," Wayne chirped. "She never loses reports . . . uh . . . like this one." He held up a form that had fallen to the floor.

Chris snarled, then grabbed the report from Wayne and began rolling it into the typewriter with his one good hand.

"What are you kids doing here anyway?" he asked.

"Sorry about your arm, Chris," I said in my most sincere voice.

"Yeah, me too," Wayne added. Only *he* didn't sound very sincere.

"Sure, sure you are. As I recall, the last thing I heard Saturday as they whisked me off in the ambulance was your big loud mouth laughing."

Wayne had to bite his lip to keep from giggling, and turned away.

"Chris, do you know where my uncle Roy went?" I asked, trying to change the subject.

"Yep. He took that no-'count nag back to Major Stiles. That stupid horse. Good thing your uncle Roy left before I got here today. I was about ready to tear that horse apart with my bare hands."

"Uh, don't you mean your bare *hand*?" Wayne corrected.

"Ah, get outa here, you punk." Chris threw a magazine at Wayne, who ducked just before it hit the wall and slid to the floor.

"Chris," I interrupted before he could toss another one. "Do you know where Major Stiles lives?"

"All I know is that it's a little house with a one-stall barn on the other side of Memorial Park, just a couple of miles from here. The old major hated to give up his precious grand champion in the first place, but he's got bad arthritis and can't take care of him anymore. I wonder what he thinks of his prizewinner now?"

I grabbed the Houston white pages and flipped through it until I found some Stileses. I saw a Maj. T. M. Stiles on Perkins Street. That street sounded familiar, so I was sure I could find it.

"Let's go find Skyjacker," I said to Wayne.

"Better hurry, boys," Chris popped off. "Old Major Stiles said he can't take care of that horse. Guess he'll just have to sell Skyjacker to the glue factory."

Then Chris threw back his head and laughed as we scrambled out the door.

THE MAJOR

I had to practically drag Wayne to our bikes. He wanted to pick a handful of green acorns and ambush Chris at his desk. I finally convinced him that we didn't have time. It would probably take us an hour to find Major Stiles's house.

The first thing we did was pedal down to the Exxon station a block from the police stables. They had a big city map stretched out across one wall. We studied it, and saw that Perkins Street was on the other side of Memorial Park. But Memorial was the biggest park in town. It had bike trails, jogging trails, a public swimming pool, tennis courts, two or three baseball fields, and even a golf course. After twenty minutes of pedaling, we still hadn't reached the other side.

"Well, shoot!" Wayne said as we paused and stared at the endless pine trees around us. "It must be on the other side of the golf course. Let's keep going."

We passed the country club, where the golfers rented their little carts, then one of the baseball diamonds. We followed the park road until we suddenly saw a small subdivision of old wooden houses and brick cottages with big pine trees and dried needles all over their front yards.

"Look! There's Perkins Street!" Wayne shouted.

I wiped the sweat off my neck and forehead, then sighed with relief. We began looking for Major Stiles's house, and before long I saw it: a tidy asbestos-shingle house painted yellow, with a black iron fence in front and a closed wooden corral in back. As soon as we rode up, I heard Skyjacker whinny.

"He knows we're here," I said.

We went around back, and Skyjacker came trotting up, his ears pointed and his tail waving.

He never looked more beautiful, but the corral was so small, he seemed to cross it in one or two strides. I couldn't wait to feel his soft muzzle and pet his head. I climbed up on the fence, leaned over as far as I could, then slapped his neck.

"Hey, boy. I sure did miss you," I said.

Wayne gave Skyjacker a few pats on the neck, then crawled over the fence and began snooping around the little lean-to that served as a one-horse stall and storage room.

"Better be careful, Wayne. We should go knock on the front door and ask permission to be back here."

The words were hardly out of my mouth when we heard a man's gruff voice.

"What're you boys doing with my horse! Get down from there! Can't you read the no-trespassing sign? Get down or I'll call the police."

I jumped about two feet and slid down the fence. Wayne made a dart for the fence and scrambled back over it.

I turned and saw an old man whose gray hair was cut in a flattop. He wore tan khakis and had

a baseball bat gripped in one hand, and was leaning on a cane with the other. Little wire-rimmed
glasses rested on a big round nose.

"You! March up here," he ordered.

I swallowed and looked around for Wayne, but
he was safely out of sight. Probably halfway
across the park by now. I hung my head and crept
closer.

"What're you doing out there?"

"I was just petting Skyjacker."

"How'd you know his name?"

"My uncle Roy is the trainer over at the police-
horse stables. I took care of Skyjacker for a few
days until . . . until the accident."

"Hmmmph!" The old man glared a few more
minutes, his chin kinda quivering. Then he low-
ered the bat.

"So you took a fancy to Skyjacker, did ya?"

I nodded. "He's the best horse I've ever seen."

"You think so, huh? Well, come on inside and
let me show you something." He pushed the back
screen door and held it open. I glanced around,
hesitating.

"And you out there behind the tree might as well come in and have a look too!" the major shouted. I turned around and looked, but didn't see anything. Sure enough, after a moment Wayne peeped around a big pine tree, dusted off his pants, and stepped up onto the porch.

"Howdy," he said to the major. "Nice place."

We followed the old man inside, watched him put his bat behind the door, then trailed him into a wood-paneled room. It was what my mother always calls a den. It had an old stone fireplace, stuffed animal heads on the walls, and pictures of military stuff. A collection of antique firearms sat under a long glass case.

"Looky here. That's what I wanted to show you boys." The major pointed to another wall. The paneling had come loose at some of the seams and it was all buckled, but it was covered with blue ribbons and trophies and photos of horses jumping over hedges or white fences.

"Wow!" I said, and leaned closer. "Is that one Skyjacker?"

"No. That's Skyjacker's grandsire. He was one

of the best jumpers the army riding team ever had. We took many a trophy together." The old man lovingly studied the photos.

"You're the man in all these photos?" Wayne asked.

"Well, not all of them. All of the black-and-whites, and some of the color pictures. When I was a young whippersnapper." He chuckled, and ran his hand over one of the old photos.

"Later, I just trained jumpers. That's my son on Skyjacker's sire."

"Why doesn't your son take care of Sky-jacker?" I asked.

"Oh, he got too busy. Landed an important job with the diplomatic corps and moved overseas. No time for riding anymore. No time for a wife and kids, either. He left Skyjacker here with me."

I looked at Wayne and knew he was thinking what I was thinking. But I asked the question first.

"Major Stiles, how are you going to take care of Skyjacker?"

"Well, that's why I donated him to the police. Figured they could use a well-trained horse. Skyjacker's only six years old. Still has plenty of good years left. He has a great temperament. I can't believe he threw a young police officer. I just don't understand it."

I coughed, and Wayne stepped up and slapped my back.

"Need a drink, boys? I've got some soda pops in the icebox," the old man said.

We nodded, and followed him into a tiny kitchen with pale-blue ceramic-tile countertops. He gave each of us a can of that off-brand stuff, and took an orange soda for himself.

"Too bad I'll have to get rid of Skyjacker now. I can't handle him alone, and I can't afford to hire somebody. Not on my Social Security and pension."

Wayne looked at me, and I nodded.

"Major Stiles," I said, "we'll look after Skyjacker for you."

"What? Well, I don't have much money. The horse feed and hay takes every extra penny I've got."

"We don't mind. We like Skyjacker."

"You'll have to feed him every day. Clean out the stable, brush him, and exercise him every day too. It's a lot of responsibility."

"We don't mind," I said again. "I'll do all the feeding and grooming, and Wayne can exercise him over in the park."

Major Stiles squinted behind his glasses, then grinned.

"All right. I'll keep him for the summer. But when school starts, you won't have time. I'll have to sell him one way or another."

I didn't like that thought, but it was only the end of May, and next fall seemed a long, long way off. So we gladly agreed. Only Wayne was more glad than me, because I finally said I wouldn't squeal to Uncle Roy about the cockle-bur. Not for a while. Not as long as Skyjacker was mine to take care of. But the end of the summer would be another story.

9

BAYOU BLUES

After school was out for the summer, I thought I'd have plenty of time for taking care of Skyjacker. But things didn't work out that way.

Wayne decided that if we stopped showing up at the police stables, Uncle Roy would get suspicious.

"It's the same thing as admitting we're guilty," he reasoned.

I'd be over at the major's place by eight o'clock, feeding and watering Skyjacker, then at the police stables to meet Wayne by nine. After lunch I'd help my sister with her baby-sitting job.

Then, in the late afternoon, I'd meet Wayne

at Major Stiles's and feed Skyjacker again and clean the stable. Then Wayne would saddle and bridle Skyjacker, and exercise him through the park, down the riding trails. I'd turn green with envy, wishing I had the nerve to ride like that. Wayne didn't make fun of me, but I always felt like a chicken. So one day I finally decided I'd try it, no matter what.

I rode Skyjacker around the little paddock and it wasn't so bad. The next day Wayne brought his fishing gear, and we asked Major Stiles if we could ride Skyjacker over to Buffalo Bayou and fish off the banks.

The ride over there was fun. We took it nice and easy. Lots of people stared, but mostly they waved and smiled. A couple of cars honked, but Skyjacker didn't flinch a muscle. Nothing bothered him.

We caught a couple of little catfish, but let them go.

"Wayne, don't you think enough time's gone by?" I asked when we were packing up to leave. "Maybe we should tell Uncle Roy what really happened."

Wayne looked brokenhearted, then shrugged.

"I thought we decided not to tell until the summer was over. I thought you liked taking care of Skyjacker."

"I do. But every time I go into the police stables and see his empty stall or see Chris Parker in his sling, I think about how much everybody thinks Skyjacker is a no-'count, good-for-nothing coward. It really gets to me."

Wayne hated it when I talked like that. He skidded a handful of rocks across the bayou.

"Do what you want, Brandon. I'm going to Astroworld tomorrow to try out the new Super Twister roller coaster. You can tell Uncle Roy if you like. If you do, I won't be coming around to help you anymore."

Then Wayne grabbed his fishing gear and jumped up on Skyjacker.

"Let's ride back real fast!" he shouted down, and held out his hand. "I feel like having the wind in my face."

Sometimes Wayne could be a complete jerk, and I told him so.

He just said, "See you back at the stables," and off he charged.

I got so mad, I saw red all the way back to Major Stiles's. Wayne really could be a pain in the neck sometimes. But I couldn't imagine taking care of Skyjacker by myself. Nobody would exercise him, and he'd get all out of shape. Then I got mad at Wayne because he knew I didn't have enough money saved up yet for Astroworld, and he was going without me. He wasn't at Major Stiles's when I got there, but I didn't even care.

The next morning, at the police stables, I decided to tell Uncle Roy. When I walked inside the stables, there were Uncle Roy and Chris Parker, with his arm still in the sling. They were talking about the upcoming Fourth of July parade. Every horse on the mounted patrol would be downtown doing crowd control during the parade and festivities.

Chris saw me, then grinned and took a swipe at my hair.

"Where's Wayne-the-Pain?" he asked.

"He went to Astroworld."

"Without you?"

"I've got too many chores to do."

Uncle Roy leaned on a stall door and looked right at me.

"What are you two boys up to every afternoon, anyhow?" he asked. "Your mom says you disappear every afternoon."

"Oh, just playing around with Wayne. Yesterday we went fishing. Caught two catfish."

"Hmmm." Uncle Roy pushed back his hat. "She says sometimes your clothes are all covered with dirt and smelling like a horse."

"Uh, well . . . we play in the dirt a lot."

"That's funny. Major Stiles tells me he has two fine young boys taking care of Skyjacker now. They fit your descriptions perfectly."

I swallowed, then grinned.

"Okay, I confess. We are taking care of Skyjacker. He's the best horse I've ever seen."

"Ha!" Chris Parker popped off. "He's a gun-shy fool. If I ever see him again, I'm gonna get out my baseball bat and knock some sense into him."

"That's not fair, Chris. He's real gentle. I've been riding him myself."

"Well . . . that's news," Uncle Roy said.

"Nothing bothers him, not even a backfiring car. Why don't you give him another chance? Maybe he was just feeling sick when he threw Chris."

"Well, maybe so. But we have to have a horse that can be counted on *all* the time, not just when he feels like it. If he went wild in the middle of a crowd, you can't imagine the damage he might do."

I felt all sick inside. I wanted to confess and get it over with, but it didn't seem right without Wayne there to help out. And the look in Chris Parker's eyes when he talked about Skyjacker was scary.

When I got home, I didn't even feel like eating lunch or helping my sister. I just wanted to crawl under the bedcovers and sleep all day. I fell asleep, then woke up to a loud ringing. I thought it was the alarm clock, because it was six and time to go feed Skyjacker, but it was the telephone.

I picked up the receiver and recognized Wayne's voice.

"Well, did you tell Uncle Roy about the cocklebur?" He sounded unsure, like he couldn't decide whether to be glad or mad.

"No." I sighed. "I tried, but Chris was there bad-mouthing Skyjacker." Then I heard a whinny in the background. "Where are you?"

"I'm at the major's. Come on over. I've got some great news."

"About Skyjacker?"

"Yep."

I put on my sneakers and tore out of the apartment door. It was about time something good happened.

WAYNE'S SURPRISE

When I got to the major's stable, I saw that Wayne hadn't even fed or watered Skyjacker yet. I guessed he was waiting for me to do it. He was down on the ground fiddling with something and had a brown paper sack in one hand.

"What are you doing back from Astroworld so soon? I figured you'd be there till closing time."

"Ah, it was no fun without you. My aunt and uncle and parents came along, and my bratty little cousin and sister, but they were so b-o-r-i-n-g. But look at what I've got." He held up the sack. I could see three long wires sticking out of the top.

"Fireworks?"

"Yep. We stopped at that little barbeque place on the outside of town. You know, the one we took you to once? My dad loves their spareribs. There's a fireworks stand next door."

"Yeah, I remember. But I didn't think your folks liked you to have fireworks. They're illegal inside the city limits."

Wayne grinned. "Who says my parents know about it? Besides, we can shoot them out over the water so nothing will catch on fire. It'll be safe."

"Okay. But why did you bring the fireworks here? What if Major Stiles sees them?"

"He won't. He left a while before you got here. I just wanted to show you what I bought."

Maybe Wayne was telling the truth, but I didn't like the way he was unwrapping the paper on the pack of Black Cats. And when I saw him slip a Bic lighter from his pocket, I knew we were in trouble.

"Hey, Wayne, is this why you called me? You said you had some good news about Skyjacker, didn't you?"

He held the lighter in midair, then put out the flame and stuck it back in his pocket.

"Oh, yeah, I almost forgot. I was talking to Major Stiles before he left. You know the Fourth of July parade downtown tomorrow morning?"

"Sure. Uncle Roy and Chris were just talking about it."

"Well, here's the good news. Major Stiles said you and me can ride Skyjacker in the parade. His VFW post is having a few horses in it, and the major said we could go in his place because he doesn't feel up to it this year. Won't that be great?"

"Ride in the parade?"

"Come on. It'll be terrific. We can dress up in costumes. How about those cowboy clothes we wore to the rodeo last February? And Major Stiles has a big American flag he wants us to carry."

"I don't know. . . ."

"Look—I'll sit in front, and you won't have to do any of the reining. Just hold on to me. It'll be all right. You know I'm a good rider, and

Skyjacker is perfect. He'd never do anything crazy. You're always saying that yourself."

I began to picture the parade, with its floats made of red-white-and-blue flowers, and the marching bands from local schools. My sister was going to be in it. She played the piccolo for the high-school band.

"All right, Wayne. I'll ask Mom. But you've got to promise me—no crazy stuff."

"Okay. It's a deal." We shook hands.

It was getting late, so I fed, watered, and groomed Skyjacker, and then cleaned the stable while Wayne rode him around the tiny corral. It was too late to take him to the park today, because we both had to be home by dark.

"Here, you ride Skyjacker a few minutes at a walk to cool him off," Wayne said after he'd run Skyjacker a few times around the corral. He gave me a leg up into the saddle.

It felt great to be on top of Skyjacker, as long as he didn't trot or suddenly gallop. But I trusted him. He would never run away with me. Still, the fear of him suddenly bolting over the fence and tearing down the street always hovered in the back of my brain, just like the fear of a pop quiz when you forgot to study.

I walked Skyjacker around real slow, patting his neck and talking to him. I wasn't paying any attention to Wayne, because he'd sort of disappeared into the shadows of the oak trees.

Suddenly I heard a hissing noise. Skyjacker's ears shot up like pointed spears. The noise sounded familiar, but I couldn't quite place it. Then I looked toward the shadows and saw a twinkling gold spark.

"What the . . ."

But it was too late. My words were cut off by an explosion like machine-gun fire. The ground was alive with Black Cat firecrackers popping and jumping and spitting.

I pulled up the reins, grabbed the saddle horn, and braced myself for what I knew Skyjacker was about to do.

SKYJACKER
AND THE FIRECRACKER

Skyjacker just stood there, behaving like an angel. Oh, he twitched his ears back and forth and danced a little jig, and snorted a few times, but he didn't run or buck or do anything that might hurt me.

First a big wave of relief flooded over me when the firecrackers finally sputtered out. Then an even bigger wave of anger flooded over me when I saw Wayne buckled over with laughter, pointing at me.

"You . . . you should see the expression on your face!" He dropped to his knees and laughed and laughed.

"It's not funny, Wayne!" I yelped like a hurt

dog. "I could have been killed." I slid down from the saddle, and stumbled around when I landed on my shaky legs. I could feel my face getting hotter.

"That was a rotten trick!"

"Ah, come on, be a sport," Wayne said as I grabbed the reins and led Skyjacker to the stall. I unsaddled and unbridled him, then gave him an extra handful of oats to make up for all the trouble he'd had to suffer. When Wayne came inside and tried to slap my back, I jerked my shoulder away.

"Keep away from me, Wayne. I'm warning you."

"Ah, don't be such a fraidycat, Brandon. It was just a few firecrackers. You make it sound like I was shooting at you or something."

"It's not just me. What about Skyjacker? You could've scared him so much, he might've tried to jump the fence. He could have landed in a gopher hole and broken his leg, or run down the street and gotten hit by a car. That was about the stupidest thing I ever saw you do. Maybe even more stupid than the cocklebur trick."

I was spitting mad now and didn't care if I hurt Wayne's feelings. He sure hadn't been acting like my best friend lately, and this topped the cake.

"Hey, listen, Brandon. I'm not stupid. Do you think I would have done that if I wasn't sure Skyjacker would behave?"

"Well, you sure took a chance, didn't you?"

"Nope, I didn't. Before you came over, and after the major left, I lit a few firecrackers near Skyjacker to test him. He was a perfect gentleman. Never bucked or flinched. Now I'm sure Skyjacker could pass the stress training at the stables. And after the parade tomorrow, I intend to tell your uncle Roy everything, and prove it by lighting some firecrackers right under Skyjacker's feet."

I didn't know whether to believe Wayne or not. It wouldn't have been the first time he'd stretched the truth to cover his tracks. But I guessed I wanted to believe him, so I smiled, even though I didn't mean to.

We shook on it, then parted. Later Wayne called and asked to spend the night. He brought over his cowboy clothes. They were great. He even had a pair of silver spurs on his real lizard boots.

We stayed up late, and Wayne fell asleep before I did. Somehow I kept thinking about Skyjacker in the parade, all decked out and with us carrying the flag. I hoped that Uncle Roy would see us. If some kid lit a firecracker, or somebody honked a horn in our faces, it would be proof to Uncle Roy that Skyjacker was really about the most noble horse on earth.

This time Skyjacker would not lose face. I had to make sure of it, no matter what.

HI, HO, SKYJACKER

The morning of July fourth, my mom fixed pancakes and syrup for breakfast, and by seven o'clock we were at the major's, all decked out in cowboy outfits. We ran some red-white-and-blue crepe streamers around Skyjacker's reins and saddle, then started off toward downtown, a few miles away.

We sure got a lot of strange looks from Major Stiles's neighbors and from people in cars. One lady made us stop so she could take our picture. It was already hot, hot, hot, with no breeze in a cloudless sky. I was carrying Major Stiles's big American flag on a short pole, and it kept falling over into my face until I learned how to hold it out to the side and let the wind created by walking catch it.

"Which way are we going?" I asked Wayne, who seemed to know exactly what he was doing.

"A bunch of horses and floats and stuff are going to meet on the other side of Allen Parkway. Let's just follow Memorial Drive all the way into town."

We rode toward Westcott Street, which cuts over to Memorial Drive. Only eight o'clock, and already the beads of sweat were popping out on my forehead and dripping down my neck. Wayne must have been reading my mind, because suddenly he pulled Skyjacker toward a Red Ranger convenience store.

"Let's stop and buy a Super-Giant drink. We're going to be out in this sun for hours," Wayne said.

"Yeah. Good thing we've got on cowboy hats for shade."

Wayne clicked his tongue and urged Skyjacker across the street to the store.

"I'll stay with Skyjacker while you go inside," I said, and he climbed down. But no sooner was

Wayne out of the saddle when a man in blue jogging shorts ran out of the store like a scared rabbit. He smacked into Skyjacker and looked up.

I nearly choked when I saw his face. It was covered with a stocking so that you couldn't tell anything about his features. Around his waist was a black jogger's pouch, and in his right hand was a pistol. His long black hair was pulled back in a ponytail.

We stared at each other a second. Then the man cursed under his breath and took off in the direction we had just come from. I saw him jerk off the stocking and sling it into the bushes. From behind he looked just like any other jogger going toward the park.

Then we saw a man in a red uniform come running out of the store, carrying a shotgun.

Boom! The shotgun fired, missing the robber by a mile. But it didn't miss the windshield of a parked car. Glass rained all over the parking lot. A couple of women who were standing nearby started screaming bloody murder, but Skyjacker didn't budge. He just twitched his ears a little.

Then the car owner came running out of the store, shouting in Spanish and shaking his fists at the store owner.

"Stop that thief!" yelled the owner, waving his empty shotgun and cursing. "That's the third time he's robbed me."

Wayne leaped back up on Skyjacker and spun him around fast. Then he shouted down to the owner, "Call 911. Tell the police the Ponytail Bandit is heading down Arnot Street toward Memorial Park. He's wearing blue jogging shorts. We'll try to follow him."

"Wayne, are you craz—"

The words rolled back into my mouth as Wayne jammed his heels into Skyjacker's flanks and shouted, "Go!"

I felt myself falling backward and, with a shout, grabbed Wayne's waist and held on for dear life. Wayne had done a lot of nutty things since I'd known him. But I didn't think even Wayne would be crazy enough to chase after a thief with a gun.

Up ahead the robber was running like a mad

dog, looking behind him and dodging the traffic that was honking and shouting and squealing brakes.

"He's heading for the parking lot over by the baseball diamonds. If he gets into that crowd, we'll never find him," Wayne said over his shoulder. "I'm going to cut him off and make him go down the joggers' trail." Suddenly Wayne turned Skyjacker toward a small offshoot of the park, filled with tall pines and oak trees.

"We can't go through there!" I screamed. "There are too many trees. We'll get our heads knocked off!"

"Just keep low!" Wayne yelled back, and made Skyjacker cut between the trees like an expert cow horse cutting calves from a herd. First to the left, then to the right, always toward the thief.

Then I heard a loud noise and saw fire spit from the man's hand. A tree limb fell a few inches from our heads.

"He's shooting at us!" I screamed.

"Duck lower!" Wayne called back, and we both leaned over so that Skyjacker's neck was blocking off a lot of the wind.

The robber saw Skyjacker bearing down on him and did exactly what Wayne wanted. He gave up going toward the parking lot and turned left. He hit the jogging trail at a full run, then vanished around a bend in the path. When we came around the bend, Wayne pulled Skyjacker to a halt.

"He's gone!" we both said in unison.

Wayne took Skyjacker farther on down the jogging trail, but as far as we could see, the trail had only joggers in red or green or pink shorts. And none had ponytails, except the girls.

"Where could he be?" I asked.

"He musta cut into the woods," Wayne said.

"I saw a little service road back there," I said.

Wayne turned the horse around and went back to where the thief had vanished.

"Look!" I shouted. "There he is."

I pointed at a small road that cut a dusty white line through the dense woods. At the very end I saw the flag of a golf course and a man in blue jogging shorts.

"What're we gonna do?" I called out as I looked at the tall metal gate blocking the road.

A sign on the fence next to it read: SERVICE ROAD—AUTHORIZED VEHICLES ONLY.

Wayne didn't answer. That was bad news, real bad news. He backed Skyjacker up all the way to Memorial Loop Road, about a hundred feet away. My heart began to pound. I didn't even want to ask him what he had in mind.

"Hold on tight!" he said, but he didn't have to tell me that. I grabbed his waist and clenched my legs as hard as I could as Skyjacker began running toward the tall metal gate. I couldn't stand to look. I closed my eyes and pressed my face against Wayne's back. The hooves pounded until my head was about to bust. Then we were up in the air, sailing over the gate like it was nothing. We landed with a little jolt, and then the hooves started pounding again.

Squirrels scampered out of our way and trees flew by in a blur until we reached the golf course, specked with a few early-morning golfers. We saw a splash of blue jogging shorts and a ponytail running across the seventeenth green.

Three golfers turned and stared, first at the

running man, then at the running horse. We were heading straight for them.

Suddenly the Ponytail Bandit stopped, turned, and fired his gun at us. The golfers shrieked and jumped into a sand trap. Just as they raised their heads up, here came Skyjacker. The men screamed again when Skyjacker leaped over the sand pit, just inches over their heads.

I glanced behind us and saw big chunks of pretty green grass spewing up under Skyjacker's hooves. Boy, some gardener was really going to be mad.

By the time we reached the edge of the fairway, we could hear sirens. They seemed to be coming from every direction, circling around the golf course on the Loop Road. The thief was really starting to get tired. He stopped again and fired at us, this time hitting a little pine tree. He cut through some more trees and headed toward the clubhouse parking lot. He fired again, and again. We kept ducking, and tried to keep some trees between him and us. He fired one last time, then threw his empty gun away.

We were just about to catch up with him when we passed under a low pine-tree branch. It wasn't very big, but I heard it hit Wayne, and he groaned.

"Wayne! Are you all right?"

Wayne didn't answer, but I could feel him slipping from the saddle. I reached around his waist and took the reins, but couldn't get a good enough grip to pull them.

Then I saw the robber heading straight for a row of cars parked along the Loop Road. Flashing red-and-blue lights were coming from both directions of the road. But they'd better hurry, or the thief would get lost in the crowd of baseball fans and picnickers who were running to see what the commotion was all about.

Then the robber squeezed between two parked cars. There was no way Skyjacker could get between them, because he was too big. Now he would *have* to stop.

Boy, was I wrong! Skyjacker charged at the cars at a full gallop, suddenly coiled his muscles, and sailed through the air like a Frisbee. His hooves hit the asphalt with a loud clank. The thief looked up, then held his hands over his face and screamed as the big red horse knocked him to the pavement. I could feel Wayne slipping off the saddle, and tried to hold him up and get the flag untangled from around my legs.

Five policemen rushed over and snapped hand-cuffs on the robber.

Two more cops rushed up to me and Wayne.

"This boy's hurt," said one of them. "Better call an ambulance."

They helped Wayne down. He was groaning and holding his head. Blood was all over his fingers. But after one of the policemen wiped it clean with his handkerchief, the cop smiled.

"He'll be all right. Just nicked in the head."

They patted Wayne and me on the back, and people all around us began snapping pictures. I saw a TV-station van, and a couple of reporters with a camera coming toward us. They pointed it at Wayne and held a microphone up to his face. One cameraman wanted a photo of me and Skyjacker. He lifted his camera at us, then looked kinda of funny.

"Say, has anybody called a doctor yet?"

"Oh, Wayne's all right. Just a graze. The ambulance will be here soon."

"I wasn't talking about a doctor for the kid, sonny. What you need is a veterinarian. That horse has been shot."

I whirled around and looked where he was pointing. A big stream of blood was oozing from Skyjacker's right shoulder.

THE HEROES

When I saw that bullet hole, I felt sick inside.

"Skyjacker" was all I could say. Then I stroked his chest and neck. He was hot and sweaty, and I knew he needed a blanket and cooling off. I grabbed the only thing I had, the big American flag, which had gotten all wrapped around its pole, and tossed it over Skyjacker. Then I walked him over to the police sergeant's squad car.

"Sergeant, we have to call for a veterinarian. This horse is hurt real bad."

"Hmmm," he said. "It'll take a long time for a vet to get over here, with all the traffic snarled up because of the parade downtown."

Suddenly an idea popped into my head.

"Then call the mounted police stables. They're just on the other side of the park. My uncle Roy works there. Tell him to bring a horse trailer so we can haul a wounded horse to the vet."

The sergeant smiled.

"Smart kid," he said, then pressed the button on his car radio.

"Patch me through to the mounted-police stables, Sally. Ask for Roy." The static crackled; then a familiar voice answered.

"This is the police stables." It was Uncle Roy himself speaking. Boy, was I relieved.

"We've got a horse wounded over here in a holdup attempt. We need you to bring a trailer on over to Memorial Park in front of the country club."

"Which horse is it?"

"It's not one of yours. Belongs to a couple of kids. They chased down a robber. The horse jumped clean over a car and knocked him down. We've got a real hero on our hands here."

"Well, I'll be doggone," Uncle Roy said.

I could hear the surprise in his voice even over

the radio. But that was nothing compared to what he was going to say when he saw it was me, Wayne, and Skyjacker. And of course, I knew he'd tell my mom. There was no way out of that. Suddenly I felt even sicker than before and had to sit down on the squad-car bumper.

It took Uncle Roy only a few minutes to get there. I was right. The look on his face when he saw us just about took the cake. He was speechless.

After he'd loaded Skyjacker into the one-horse trailer, he laid his big hands on my shoulders.

"Brandon, do you want to ride with me to the vet?"

He didn't have to say anything else. I knew what he was really asking. Did I want to go along, just in case Skyjacker died? Big tears swelled up in my eyes and I could hardly see how to climb up into his pickup.

"Where's Wayne?" he asked. "Does he want to come along?"

"He's over there," I said, and pointed toward the crowd. We could see the top of Wayne's hair and hear the click of cameras going off. Then I saw Wayne making motions like he was reliving the chase, and the TV reporters were laughing.

"I think Wayne's too busy to come with us," I said.

Uncle Roy lifted out one of those portable sirens and stuck it on top of his pickup. It would have been fun under normal circumstances to watch the cars scatter out of the way and see people on the sidewalks staring. But these weren't normal conditions, and all I could think about was poor Skyjacker bleeding and hurting all because Wayne had to be a hero.

"You know, Brandon, I would have never guessed it was you and Wayne chasing down that Ponytail Bandit. You feel better about riding Skyjacker now, don't you?"

I nodded. "I guess so. I wasn't even thinking about it when we were chasing that guy. I was more worried about the bullets and about Skyjacker running into a tree. I guess after that chase, riding at a normal gallop will be a piece of cake."

"There's another thing," said Uncle Roy. "Skyjacker. I wonder why he got so brave all of a sudden, going after a man firing a gun? And keeping after him even when he took a bullet in the shoulder."

Uncle Roy shook his head. "Nope, I sure had this horse pegged for a gun-shy coward. And I thought I knew horses. But I guess I was wrong. What do you think made him do it, Brandon?"

I swallowed hard and looked out the window, then took a deep breath.

"Uncle Roy, I've got a confession to make."

Uncle Roy reached over and put his hand on my knee.

"I know something has been bothering you ever since Chris got thrown. Why don't you tell me what really happened?"

So I opened up and told him everything, from the time Chris stuffed the plastic snakes in the thermos jug right up to that Saturday Wayne put the cocklebur under the blanket for the third time. Then I let out a sigh.

Uncle Roy shook his head and pushed his hat back.

"Well, I figured it must have been something like that. I found some spots of dried blood on

Skyjacker's saddle blanket that Saturday, but they could have been old. What I couldn't understand was why Wayne, and especially you, would want to play such a nasty trick on Skyjacker. Seeing how much you liked him."

"It wasn't supposed to be a trick on Skyjacker, Uncle Roy. It was supposed to be a trick on Chris Parker, to get even for all those practical jokes he was playing on us."

"Sometimes jokes don't always turn out the way we like, do they? Especially when an innocent bystander—or innocent horse—is in the way."

"I'm sorry Skyjacker got fired and dishonored. I really am sorry, Uncle Roy."

"Well, maybe you and Wayne have learned your lesson. Maybe Chris Parker has too. It's a shame Skyjacker was the one who ended up getting hurt the most. Sure hope he pulls through. It would be a terrible thing to lose a good horse like that."

I shivered at his words.

We drove into the vet's parking lot. The vet

was already waiting. They rushed Skyjacker to the barn and began sticking him with needles and digging the bullet out. I couldn't stand to watch, so I curled up on the sofa inside the vet's office waiting room, praying that Skyjacker would be all right.

14

TRUCE

When I woke up, I was in my own bed and the sun was rising. My mother was standing over me, holding the morning newspaper. There on the front page was Wayne grinning and another, smaller picture of me and Skyjacker looking all confused.

"Wake up, Rip Van Winkle," my mom said. "You've been asleep since yesterday morning. All that excitement really knocked you out."

"Sleep? I didn't even know I *was* asleep."

"Come on and get dressed. Uncle Roy wants us to come down to the police stables. He's got something to tell us."

Panic rushed over me. I wanted to slip back under the covers. Was Skyjacker dead? Was

Uncle Roy going to tell my mom about the cocklebur? A jillion things popped into my head.

"Why does he want to see us?" I asked.

"Don't know. He just said to bring you and Wayne to the stables. You know your uncle; he's a man of few words."

Bring Wayne too! Now I knew we were in trouble. I dressed, and my mom had to practically drag me out the door. When we stopped by Wayne's house to pick him up, he looked about as worried as me. His mother wasn't as happy as mine, especially since Wayne had gotten a cut on his head and had gone to the doctor. He had a big patch on it now.

"I'm grounded a month," he groaned as soon as he slid into the backseat next to me. "Boy, is my dad mad. He wanted to fan my breeches and send me off to military school. But my mom talked him out of it. They only let me out because your uncle Roy called them."

"Do they know about the cocklebur?" I whispered.

"You don't think I'm gonna ask them *that* question, do ya?"

When we arrived, I couldn't believe my eyes. Every single mounted policeman was in spit-polished boots and standing at attention beside his horse. The rows stretched all the way from the parking lot to the stables. Uncle Roy looked neat as a pin, and even Major Stiles was there, dressed in his military uniform.

"What's going on?" I asked Wayne in a low voice.

"Maybe we're being arrested," he said. "Who's that woman over there in the uniform?"

"Oh, no. It's the chief of police."

My mom parked the car; then we began walking across the gravel, between the rows of policemen and their horses. I knew most of them, but no one batted an eye or smiled at us.

"Boys, come on up here," Uncle Roy said with a wave of his arm. "The chief has something to say to you."

I couldn't believe a practical joke was causing so much stink. She talked a few minutes about brave policemen going beyond the call of duty. But to tell the truth, I wasn't listening until she said her final sentence.

". . . so it gives me great honor to award this Citation of Valor to the newest member of the Houston Mounted Police—Skyjacker."

From the stables behind her came Smitty leading Skyjacker, who had a big white bandage over his wounded shoulder. Everybody broke into applause, and Wayne and I both cheered like we were at a ball game.

The chief held up a wooden plaque with a brass plate that twinkled in the sun. Skyjacker sniffed it, then shook his head just like he knew he was a hero. I couldn't help myself another minute. I ran up and threw my arms around Skyjacker's neck.

"You're alive!" I said as I stroked his face.

Next thing I knew Wayne was next to me, patting Skyjacker too.

"I told you everything would turn out okay, Brandon. I told you Skyjacker would be put back on the force. You've got to learn to trust me."

I was too silly happy to argue with Wayne this time, and just started laughing. Then I saw Chris Parker strolling up. He had something hidden behind his back and was heading straight for Wayne.

"Hey, Wayne-the-Pain," he called out. "I've got something for you."

"Oh, no you don't," Wayne said, and ducked under Skyjacker's neck. "Keep away from me."

Chris grinned his big horse-tooth smile and shook his head.

"It's just a little peace offering." He held out a brand-new pair of jeans. Wayne glanced at me and flashed the secret signal that something was up.

I shook my head. "I believe him," I whispered. "Go ahead."

Wayne took the pants gingerly, then smiled.

"Truce," Chris said, and stuck out his hand.

"Truce," Wayne replied, and shook hands.

And Chris Parker and Wayne kept their word. Neither one played a joke on the other the rest of the summer, or ever. Like I said, I never did understand why folks call those little pranks they play on each other "practical jokes." There's sure nothing practical about them. And sometimes they're a lot more trouble than they're worth. If you don't believe it, just ask Wayne. Or Chris Parker. Oh, yeah, or ask Skyjacker.